Team Stats—Football Edition

HIGHLIGHTS OF THE CHICAGO BEARS

MARYSA STORM

Black Rabbit Books

Bolt is published by Black Rabbit Books
P.O. Box 3263, Mankato, Minnesota, 56002.
www.blackrabbitbooks.com
Copyright © 2020 Black Rabbit Books

Jennifer Besel, editor; Michael Sellner, interior designer; Grant Gould, cover designer; Omay Ayres, photo researcher

All rights reserved. No part of this book may be reproduced, stored in a retrieval system or transmitted in any form or by any means, electronic, mechanical, photocopying, recording, or otherwise, without written permission from the publisher.

Library of Congress Cataloging-in-Publication Data
Names: Storm, Marysa, author.
Title: Highlights of the Chicago Bears / by Marysa Storm.
Description: Mankato, Minnesota : Black Rabbit Books, [2020] | Series: Bolt. Team stats. Football edition | Includes bibliographical references and index. | Audience: Age 8-12. | Audience: Grade 4 to 6.
Identifiers: LCCN 2018044238 (print) | LCCN 2018054734 (ebook) | ISBN 9781680728910 (ebook) | ISBN 9781680728859 (library binding) | ISBN 9781644660829 (paperback)
Subjects: LCSH: Chicago Bears (Football team)—Juvenile literature. | Football—Illinois—Chicago—History—Juvenile literature. | Football players—United States—Biography—Juvenile literature.
Classification: LCC GV956.C5 (ebook) | LCC GV956.C5 S76 2020 (print) | DDC 796.332/640977311—dc23
LC record available at https://lccn.loc.gov/2018044238

Printed in the United States of America. 1/19

Image Credits

AP Images: AP, 16 (tr), 19, 21; AP / NFHOF, 4–5; ASSOCIATED PRESS, 10; LIEBB / AP, 9; Marc Pesetsky, 23 (r); NFHOF, 22 (r), 24 (both); PHIL SANDLIN, 14–15; Ryan Kang, 28–29 (t); Vernon Biever, 20; commons.wikimedia.org: 15 (trophy); Private collection of Michael Moran, 6 (b); Dreamstime: Jerry Coli, 1; en.wikipedia.org/sterneman.net: Decatur Public Library, 6 (t); Getty: Bettmann, 12–13; Focus on Sport, 23 (l); Icon Sportswire, 3, 16–17 (bkgd); Joe Robbins, Cover; Robert Riger, 22 (l); Tony Inzerillo, 26–27; Vic Stein, 25; Zach Bolinger/Icon Sportswire, 16–17; Shutterstock: EFKS, 22–23 (bkgd); enterlinedesign, 28–29 (b); Svyatoslav Aleksandrov, 31; VitaminCo, 8, 14, 32
Every effort has been made to contact copyright holders for material reproduced in this book. Any omissions will be rectified in subsequent printings if notice is given to the publisher.

CONTENTS

CHAPTER 1
On the Field..........4

CHAPTER 2
History of
the Bears.............7

CHAPTER 3
Greatest Moments.....11

CHAPTER 4
Stars of the Bears.....18

Other Resources............30

CHAPTER 1

On the FIELD

In 1933, the NFL held its first championship game. The Chicago Bears and New York Giants faced off. In the final minutes, the Giants were ahead. But then a Bears' player passed the ball downfield. Another player made the catch. But then he quickly tossed the ball to a player near him. And that guy ran it in. *Touchdown!*

The Bears won the first championship!

1924 Team

CHAPTER 2

HISTORY of the Bears

The Bears has a long history. The team started in 1920 as the Decatur Staleys. In 1921, the team moved to Chicago. One year later, it became the Bears. The young team won many games. At one point, it had four straight championship appearances.

Da Bears

In 1982, Mike Ditka took over as coach. The Bears' power soon peaked again. In 1985, it only lost one regular-season game. The team then won the Super Bowl. The big win was the perfect end to the season.

The Bears had another big season in 2006. Again, the team went to the Super Bowl. That time, it lost.

Before coaching, Ditka was a pro football tight end.

December 8, 1940
Chicago Bears vs. Washington Redskins
73-0

November 7, 1954
Cleveland Browns vs. Washington Redskins
62-3

December 4, 1976
Los Angeles Rams vs. Atlanta Falcons
59-0

October 18, 2009
New England Patriots vs. Tennessee Titans
59-0

Largest Margins of Victory since 1935
(as of 2018)

CHAPTER 3

Greatest MOMENTS

The Bears has had many incredible moments. During a 1940 game, the team was unstoppable. It took on the Redskins. And it **dominated**. The Bears ended the game with 73 points. Its **opponents** didn't score once.

Taking Down the Giants (Again)

In 1963, the Bears reached the championship. Again, it took on the Giants. The Giants quickly gained the lead. But then the Bears' **defense** stepped in. It **intercepted** five passes. Thanks to the defense, the Bears won.

Bears' 1985 Season Stats

regular season score
15–1

total passes completed
237

total rushing yards
2,761

points made vs. points allowed
456–198

Winning the Big Game

The Bears' 1985 season was amazing. It was no surprise the team made it to the Super Bowl. Using its mighty defense, the team won the big game. It beat the Patriots 46–10. With this win, the Bears ended one of the greatest NFL seasons.

BY THE NUMBERS
(as of 2018)

14 number of retired uniform numbers

28 number of players in the Pro Football Hall of Fame

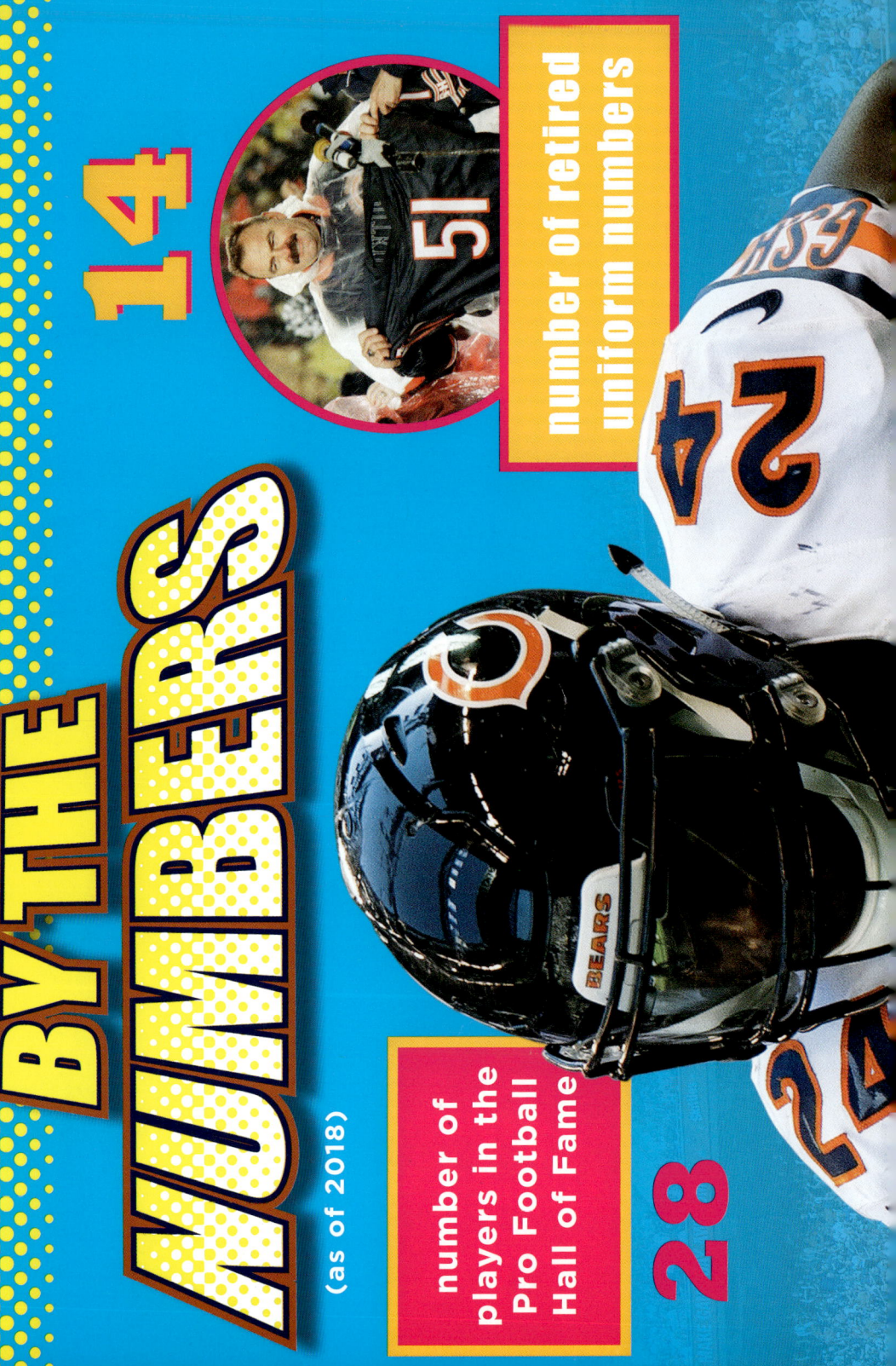

CHAPTER 4

STARS of the Bears

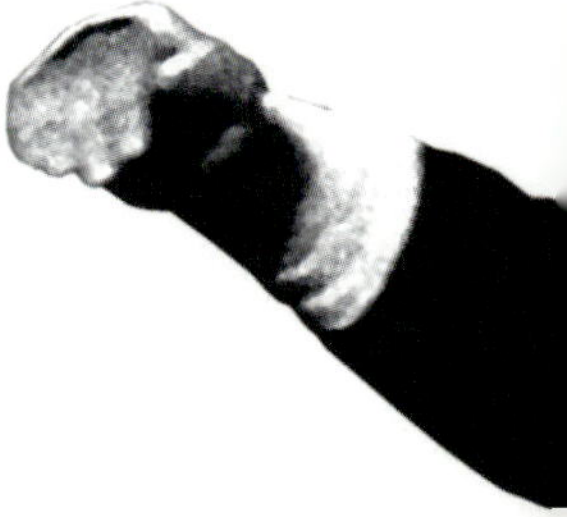

The Bears' greatest moments wouldn't have been possible without amazing players.

Intimidating and powerful, Dick Butkus played as Bears' linebacker for nine seasons. He recovered 25 **fumbles**. He made 22 interceptions. Butkus also took the ball away from opposing players 47 times.

One of Butkus' nicknames was Robot of Destruction.

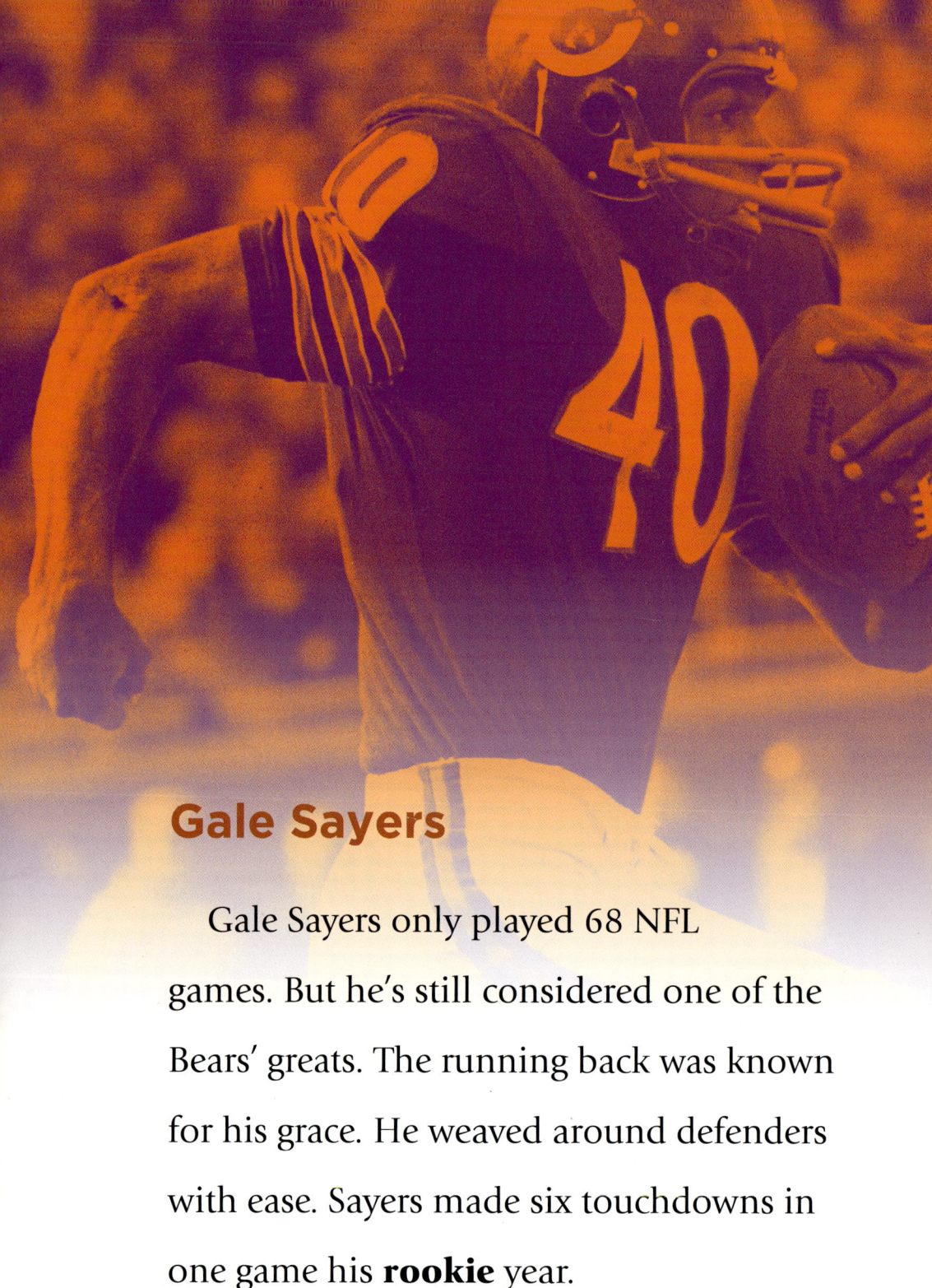

Gale Sayers

Gale Sayers only played 68 NFL games. But he's still considered one of the Bears' greats. The running back was known for his grace. He weaved around defenders with ease. Sayers made six touchdowns in one game his **rookie** year.

George Halas

George Halas was the team's first head coach. He led it a total of 40 years. Halas coached the team to many big wins. Many people call him the NFL's best coach.

Halas also owned, played for, and managed the team.

GREATEST COACHES
Halas has many impressive stats. Compare him with other great NFL coaches.

George Halas
(Bears)

years spent coaching pro football: **40**

total regular season wins: **318**

play-off record: **6–3**

championships won: **6**

CURLY LAMBEAU

GEORGE HALAS

Curly Lambeau (Cardinals, Packers, and Redskins)	Tom Landry (Cowboys)	Don Shula (Colts and Dolphins)
33	29	33
226	250	328
3–2	20–16	19–17
6	2	2

TOM LANDRY

DON SHULA

Luckman's Records

first quarterback to throw more than 400 yards in one game

threw seven touchdowns in one game

most touchdowns per attempt

Sid Luckman

For 12 years, Sid Luckman played quarterback. He held many records. After retiring from playing, he continued working with the Bears. He became a part-time assistant coach.

Walter Payton

Walter Payton was running back for the Bears. He was powerful and **agile**. It was nearly impossible to take him down. He made 125 total touchdowns in 13 seasons.

Over the years, the Bears has had many amazing players. The team has won many incredible games too. Fans enjoy looking back on these moments. And they look forward to more to come.

1968 Halas retires.

1986 Team wins its first Super Bowl.

2007 Bears play its second Super Bowl.

2018 The 28th Bears' player is inducted into the Pro Football Hall of Fame.

2020

GLOSSARY

agile (AJ-ahyl)—able to move quickly and easily

defense (DEE-fens)—the players on a team who try to stop the other team from scoring

dominate (DOM-uh-neyt)—to hold a commanding position over

fumble (FUM-buhl)—a ball that is loose because a player failed to hold on to it

intercept (in-tur-SEPT)—to catch a pass made by the other team

intimidating (in-TIM-uh-day-ting)—causing feelings of fear and awe

opponent (uh-POH-nunt)—a person, team, or group that is competing against another

retire (ree-TIYR)—to withdraw from use

rookie (ROOK-ee)—in the first year

LEARN MORE

BOOKS

Burgess, Zack. *Meet the Chicago Bears.* Big Picture Sports. Chicago: Norwood House Press, 2017.

Morey, Allan. *The Chicago Bears Story.* NFL Teams. Minneapolis: Bellwether Media, Inc., 2017.

Sawyer, Amy, and Katie Gillespie. *Chicago Bears.* My First NFL Book. New York: AV2 by Weigl, 2018.

WEBSITES

Chicago Bears Team Page
www.nfl.com/teams/chicagobears/profile?team=CHI

Football: National Football League
www.ducksters.com/sports/national_football_league.php

The Official Website of the Chicago Bears
www.chicagobears.com

INDEX

B
Butkus, Dick, 18, 19

D
Ditka, Mike, 8

H
Halas, George, 21, 22, 28–29
history, 4, 7, 8, 11, 12, 14, 15, 28–29

L
Luckman, Sid, 24–25

P
Payton, Walter, 26

S
Sayers, Gale, 20